Young Frederick Douglass
The Slave Who Learned to Read

Linda Walvoord Girard
paintings by Colin Bootman

Albert Whitman & Company
Morton Grove, Illinois

To my husband, Del.
L.W.G.

To my father and mother, Winfield and Agatha Bootman.
C.B.

Library of Congress Cataloging-in-Publication Data
Girard, Linda Walvoord.
Young Frederick Douglass: the slave who learned to read/written by
Linda Walvoord Girard; illustrated by Colin Bootman.
p.   cm.
ISBN 0-8075-9463-6
1. Douglass, Frederick, 1817?-1895—Childhood and youth—Juvenile
literature. 2. Abolitionists—United States—Biography—Juvenile
literature. 3. Afro-Americans—Biography—Juvenile literature.
[1. Douglass, Frederick, 1817?-1895—Childhood and youth.
2. Abolitionists. 3. Afro-Americans—Biography.] I. Bootman, Colin, ill.
II. Title.
E449.D75G56 1994
973.8'092—dc20
[B]   93-28245
                                                        CIP
                                                        AC

Text copyright © 1994 by Linda Walvoord Girard.
Illustrations copyright © 1994 by Colin Bootman.
Designed by Sandy Newell.
Published in 1994 by Albert Whitman & Company,
6340 Oakton Street, Morton Grove, Illinois 60053.
Published simultaneously in Canada
by General Publishing, Limited, Toronto.
Manufactured in Mexico.
10 9 8 7 6 5 4 3 2 1

> *My Dear Sir. there are three men now at my house — who are in great peril. — I am un well, I need your advice. Please come at once.*
>
> *D. F.*

In September 1851, Frederick Douglass wrote this "pass" to aid three escaped slaves on the Underground Railroad. They had arrived at his home in Rochester, New York, on their way to Canada. The note was sent to Samuel Porter, a white abolitionist who helped fugitives. The initials "D.F." rather than "F.D." helped to hide Douglass's identity from anyone who might discover the pass.

Porter Family Papers, Department of Rare Books and Special Collections, University of Rochester Library.

In the streets of Baltimore in 1826, young Frederick Bailey, a slave boy about eight years old, often saw whites stop blacks.

"Hey, boy, who do you belong to? Where are you going? Where's your pass?"

Any white person could stop any black person, for any reason or no reason. If the black person's answer wasn't satisfactory, he or she was in trouble.

Frederick noticed that some blacks carried papers with writing. The white person would read those marks and let the black person go.

If only I could write, Frederick thought, I could write my own pass, and go where I want.

That year, Frederick had been sent from a plantation in the country to live in a house in the city. On loan from his own master, he was the first and only slave of Hugh Auld, his wife, Sophia (or "Miz Sopha," as Frederick called her), and their son, Tommy, who was about five. Now he had a straw bed and enough to eat. He wore trousers instead of a tattered, knee-length linen shirt. Instead of scooping his meals from a trough, he sat on a chair at a dinner table. And his mistress was very kind. All this was strange and new.

Very often, after dinner, Mrs. Auld would get her Bible and read aloud. One night, when Mr. Auld was gone, she read the first part of the story of Job. Frederick was resting under the table. For the first time, he understood that the black marks on a page could tell a story. He crawled out, stood up, and gathered his courage.

He asked Miz Sopha if she would teach him to read.

Since she was getting ready to teach Tommy the ABCs anyway, Mrs. Auld quickly agreed that Frederick could listen to the lessons.

Mrs. Auld was amazed at how fast her slave pupil picked up the letters and their sounds. Soon Frederick could combine the letters and read words.

Then one day, Mr. Auld came home during a lesson. Mrs. Auld bragged that Frederick was learning to read, and wasn't it amazing? Wasn't it amusing?

Mr. Auld sent Frederick out of the room. Then he began to lecture his wife. Teaching a slave was against the law, he told her. And it was unsafe. A slave who could read would be "spoiled." He would get ideas. If he could read, he'd want to write as well, and if he could write, there was no telling what mischief he'd dream up.

Mrs. Auld said she was very sorry. Her own family did not have any slaves, and she didn't know that teaching slaves was illegal. From his listening place outside the door, Frederick heard her promise never to teach him again.

After that lecture, Mrs. Auld obeyed her husband and stopped teaching Frederick. Not only did she stop helping him, she also tried to prevent him from learning any more. When she didn't see Frederick for a while, she checked up on him. If she saw him practicing reading, she would angrily snatch the book or newspaper out of his hands.

Young as he was, Frederick understood that his master and mistress wanted slaves to stay ignorant.

Now that he knew it was forbidden, Frederick was determined to learn, no matter what! He knew he must find secret ways to teach himself.

From then on, if a newspaper was blowing about in the street, Frederick picked it up. If a child carelessly dropped a Sunday school paper on the way home from church, Frederick would find it.

If somebody left a schoolbook lying in the playground, it went home with Frederick. And on errands, he studied street names and the packages and signs in stores. He spelled things out, and his reading got smoother and faster.

When he was about twelve, a strange new word fascinated him. *Abolition*. What was that? Webster's dictionary said "abolish" meant "doing away." Doing away with what? He could tell from the newspaper articles that "abolitionists" made slave owners fighting mad. Did some white people want to end slavery, too?

White schoolboys who had become his friends told him to get a book of great speeches called the *Columbian Orator*. In that book, they said, a slave debates his master, and wins! The master admits defeat and gives the slave his freedom.

Frederick blacked boots to get the fifty cents he needed. He walked to a bookstore and bought the *Columbian Orator*. It was the first book that was his very own.

In this book, Frederick discovered eloquent speeches from history, especially the dialogue between the master and slave. In the next few years, he would read the speeches over and over until he understood them all. But could a slave truly win freedom by argument? Would whites listen if a slave spoke?

As his master, Mr. Auld, had feared, this slave had gotten ideas.

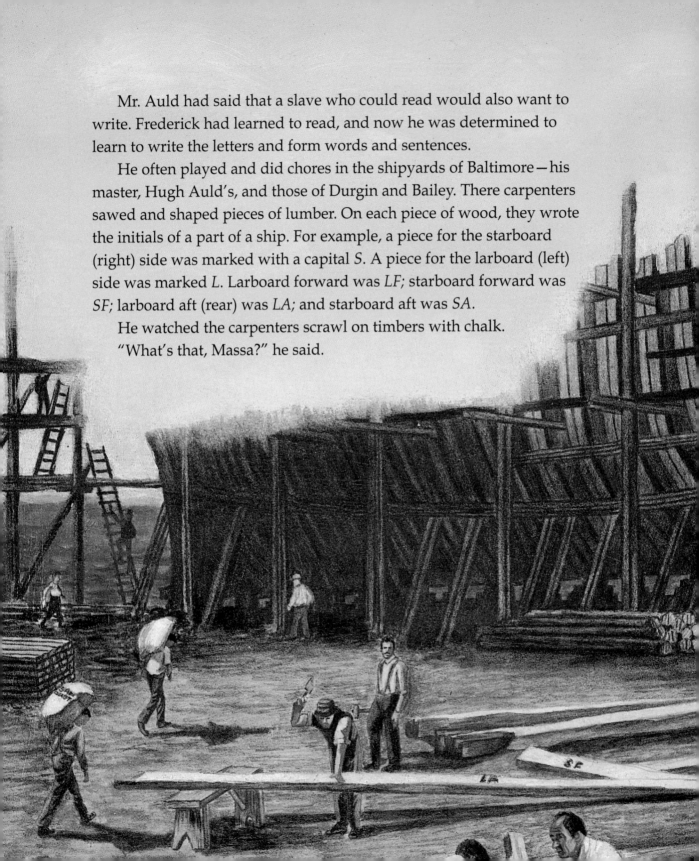

Mr. Auld had said that a slave who could read would also want to write. Frederick had learned to read, and now he was determined to learn to write the letters and form words and sentences.

He often played and did chores in the shipyards of Baltimore — his master, Hugh Auld's, and those of Durgin and Bailey. There carpenters sawed and shaped pieces of lumber. On each piece of wood, they wrote the initials of a part of a ship. For example, a piece for the starboard (right) side was marked with a capital *S*. A piece for the larboard (left) side was marked *L*. Larboard forward was *LF*; starboard forward was *SF*; larboard aft (rear) was *LA*; and starboard aft was *SA*.

He watched the carpenters scrawl on timbers with chalk.

"What's that, Massa?" he said.

"That's the letter *S*."

"Oh, the letter *S*. And what does that mean?"

"Means 'starboard.'"

"*S*, starboard. Yes, Massa, I'll remember that," he said, as he told the story many years later. "And what's that, Massa?"

"The letter *L*—'larboard.'"

"Why, I'll remember that, Massa." And so on.

Among Frederick's chores were to tend the fire that heated tar and pitch and to watch the shipyard while the carpenters went to eat. This gave him chances to copy the letters with chalk that was lying about. He knew if he could learn to make four letters, he could make the rest.

Frederick got clues from other children, too. Often, when he met white boys, he would suggest a writing contest to them. Using chalk he carried in his pocket, he drew the four letters on the pavement or on a wall. "Beat that if you can," he would say.

The other boys beat him easily, for they went to school and learned from teachers. They laughed at the idea that a slave boy could win a writing contest, and they would scrawl letters he didn't know. Frederick lost the contests. But then he would copy the new letters.

Other times, he paid for help with bread and butter he carried in his pocket. And he had made friends with a few white boys who helped him for nothing.

In the evening, in his small room above the kitchen, Frederick struggled on. He dragged a barrel up the winding stairs to make a table. There he copied the tiny letters from a hymnbook and a Bible he had found in the house. He brought leftover pieces of candles to his room and worked into the night.

To write on, he used paper scraps he found in the street. Sometimes he had to dry and clean them first. Paper was scarce, and pencils were, too. Perhaps he wrote with one of Tommy's cast-off goose quill pens.

He "borrowed" Tommy's old school copybooks — small booklets in which students practiced penmanship. Frederick made his own practice letters in the empty spaces under Tommy's writing. He could have been whipped for messing up Tommy's precious keepsake schoolbooks, but luckily he was not found out. He slipped the books back into their places, and no one ever noticed the extra writing.

By the time he was thirteen, Frederick could both read and write very well. And his knowledge *would* soon lead to trouble.

In 1832, when Frederick was about fourteen, he was given to a new master — Hugh Auld's brother, Thomas. Frederick had to leave Baltimore to live in a tiny Maryland village called St. Michael's.

He was soon punished for talking back and for stealing food. But the biggest trouble came over a Sunday school.

Other slaves learned that Frederick could read, and they asked him to teach a Sunday school. The class met secretly in a free black man's house where there were desks, spelling books, and Bibles. During the second week, Thomas Auld burst in with a white mob. The men broke up the school with clubs and threats. The whites warned the students never to meet again.

The Sunday school was the last straw for Thomas Auld. He sent Frederick for a year to a cruel slave "breaker" named Edward Covey. Frederick worked in Covey's fields from dawn to dark. Covey often whipped him for no reason. Soon Frederick's back was covered with scars, and he nearly lost an eye from a beating.

One hot summer morning, Covey started to beat him again. Frederick fought back. "I won't let you beat me," he said, over and over. Their struggle, in a hay barn, lasted two hours. To Frederick's amazement, Covey finally gave up. He never tried to beat Frederick again.

When Frederick's term with Covey ended, Auld hired him out to a much kinder master, a farmer named William Freeland. Again, Frederick started a Sunday school. Eventually he had forty students. This time he was not found out.

Not only was Frederick not learning to be a "good" slave, but he was "ruining" other people's slaves.

When Frederick was about seventeen and still working for Freeland, he made plans to run away. Four slave friends were to go with him.

Frederick wrote out five fake passes giving the slaves permission to travel. They planned to steal a canoe, paddle across the Chesapeake Bay, ditch the boat, and make their way north to freedom.

At the last minute, a slave named Sandy lost his nerve and betrayed Frederick and the others. They were arrested in the farmhouse with the fake passes in their pockets.

One of the slaves scuffled with the authorities. Meanwhile, even though his hands were tied, Frederick managed to toss his pass into the fire.

On the way to jail, the others asked Frederick what to do.

"Admit nothing," he said.

"What about our passes?"

"Eat them," he said. And they did.

Thomas Auld didn't believe Frederick had tried to escape. To Frederick's surprise, Thomas lent him back to his brother, Hugh, in Baltimore.

Frederick knew how close he had come to disaster. It would be three years before he again tried to escape. And when he did, he would go alone.

Frederick was starving for educated companionship. He joined a club of young black people called the East Baltimore Mental Improvement Society. He was the only member who was not free. And he was also one of the few members who could read. Tall and poised, the handsome Frederick Bailey stood out in this group. There he met a special, gentle young woman named Anna Murray.

Meanwhile, Hugh Auld didn't quite know what to do with Frederick. Frederick's appetite was huge, and his service was no longer needed for Tommy. Auld decided to "rent" Frederick in the shipyards. The master would collect his slave's pay.

During that year, Frederick learned the tricky task of caulking a ship—filling the seams between the planks so they would not leak. Each Friday, when he was paid, he had to hand his master his wages—at first $6.50 a week, later $9.00. This was more than some of the white dockworkers earned. Some of them felt Frederick was taking a good job, a "white" job. Once, he was severely beaten by jealous white workers. His life had become impossible.

And as long as he was a slave, he could never marry Anna. Slaves could not sign papers or make legal ties such as marriage.

Yet, Frederick was tormented when he thought of the loneliness of running away, leaving all his friends and his familiar life. If he stayed, could life in Baltimore ever be happy? He saw many free blacks moving about there, getting their own jobs, collecting their own pay. That could be his future, for Thomas Auld had promised him his freedom when he was twenty-five. But seven years was a long time to wait.

Sometimes he saw gangs of slaves who had been sold to the slave traders from Georgia or Mississippi or Louisiana. They would be sent south, shackled together in a sad line. Thomas Auld had warned him: this was his fate if he tried for freedom and failed.

In the end, Frederick could not endure slavery. When he was twenty, he made a daring new plan for escape. With money Anna lent him, he would buy a ticket and go north by public train.

But Frederick knew the conductor would question him, and so could any whites who saw him. A black person traveling north would have to show papers proving he or she was free. And "free papers" were legal documents with official seals. Frederick couldn't fake these.

A good friend, a free black sailor named Benny, loaned Frederick his sailor's "protection paper." This showed Benny was registered as a seaman with an American shipping company. Across the top of this certificate, a big American eagle spread its wings. Below was written a description of Benny.

For both Frederick and Benny, this was a risky plan. If Frederick was caught, he would be sold south into harsh slavery. And Benny could go to jail.

Frederick made his run for freedom on Monday, September 3, 1838. He promised to write Anna as soon as he was safe. Because she was free, she could come north to meet him.

Frederick planned every detail of his escape. He wore a sailor's outfit—a red shirt, a tarpaulin hat, and a black neckerchief, loosely tied. He knew it could be dangerous for a black man to wait in the station with luggage, so he hired a cab driver to race to the train with his bag and toss it to him at the very last moment.

With Benny's paper, he settled into the "Negro car" and waited for the conductor to check papers. His heart was pounding, but he acted calm.

The conductor came through and checked the papers of several free black passengers.

"I suppose you have your free papers?" he asked Frederick.

"I never carry my free papers to sea with me," said Frederick. "I have a paper with the American eagle on it that will carry me around the world." With this he pulled out the impressive-looking sailor's protection paper. The conductor never checked to see if Frederick matched the description of the paper's owner.

The trip to New York wasn't one smooth train ride. Twice the passengers had to switch to ferryboats, once in the middle of the night. And in Philadelphia, they had to get to another train station, blocks away. Frederick had to read signs and ask for directions. He was afraid of getting lost, and equally afraid of asking the wrong person for help and being reported. But his luck held. The day after he escaped, he arrived in New York City. His money was nearly gone, and he had no friends to help him.

Frederick slept on burlap sacks on the docks one night. But friendly sailors warned him he was still in danger, for the docks were patrolled for runaways. Slave owners could send agents north to find their slaves, or they could advertise in Northern papers, offering rewards to anyone who could seize their runaways and bring them back. A runaway was never completely safe anywhere in the United States.

Frederick was forced to ask a stranger for help. He chose a friendly sailor whose last name was Stewart.

Stewart took the runaway to his own home overnight. The next day, he took him to find David Ruggles, a free black abolitionist who was well known in New York.

While staying with Ruggles, Frederick wrote to Anna. She hurried north, and they were married on September 15, 1838.

For safety, Frederick changed his name from Bailey to Douglass. He had found his pass to freedom and a future as a great man.

Many slaves escaped. But none could speak, argue, or write like Frederick Douglass. The runaway slave, self-taught, soon amazed the world.

About Frederick Douglass

Frederick Douglass (1818-1895). Historians have concluded he was born in 1818, not 1817, as Douglass himself had guessed. The date of the photo is unknown.

UPI/Bettmann

After his escape, Frederick Douglass worked in a shipyard in New Bedford, Massachusetts. In his spare time, he began speaking about his life as a slave and the evil of a system that bought and sold human beings. Soon he was touring the New England states as a speaker for the Massachusetts Anti-Slavery Society. Although sometimes his speeches were two hours long, the eloquent, passionate Douglass held audiences spellbound.

Because he was so eloquent, many people did not believe that Douglass had ever been illiterate and a slave. To convince the doubters, in 1845 he published an autobiography, *Narrative of the Life of Frederick Douglass.* In it he revealed his slave name and the name and location of his master. Now he was in greater danger of being seized and returned to slavery. He left for England where he stayed for two years, giving lectures for the abolitionist cause. In 1846, English friends bought his freedom from Thomas Auld and Hugh Auld for about $700.

Narrative of the Life of Frederick Douglass quickly became a bestseller. Harriet Beecher Stowe drew on it for her famous novel, *Uncle Tom's Cabin.*

In 1847, Douglass moved with his family to Rochester, New York, and there established the *North Star*, an antislavery newspaper. He and Anna eventually had five children. Their home in Rochester was a station on the Underground Railroad, and hundreds of fugitive slaves passed through it on their way to freedom in Canada.

Throughout his adult life, Douglass worked for the rights of African Americans. He fought for job equality and for integration in schools and churches and on trains. While traveling in New England, he would sit in one of the railroad cars reserved for white passengers. Sometimes angry railroad workers would drag him out of his seat. During the Civil War, he met with Abraham Lincoln. "I know who you are, Mr. Douglass," the president told him. Lincoln had read the *North Star* when he was a young, unknown lawyer in Illinois. Now the president and the former slave discussed the slaves whom Lincoln would soon free.

From 1881 to 1886, Douglass was Recorder of Deeds in the District of Columbia, and from 1889 to 1891, he served as U.S. minister to Haiti.

Douglass wrote two more autobiographies, in 1855 and 1881. Many of his speeches and letters also exist in printed records. Every scene in this book and all quoted remarks come from Douglass's work.

The young slave who taught himself to read and write became the most important black leader of his time. Writer, orator, publisher, reformer, and statesman, Frederick Douglass died in 1895.

Linda Walvoord Girard lives near San Francisco with her husband and son. She has written ten books for Albert Whitman, including a biography of the astronomer Edmond Halley and picture books about divorce, adoption, and AIDS.

Colin Bootman, a native of Trinidad, grew up and was educated in the United States. A graduate of New York City's School of Visual Arts, he lives in the Bronx, New York, with his family. This is his first book for children.